Sports Illustrated KIDS

KNOW THE STATS

HOCKEY IS A NUMBERS GAME

by Shane Frederick

CAPSTONE PRESS
a capstone imprint

Sports Illustrated Kids Know the Stats are published by Capstone Press,
a Capstone Imprint, 1710 Roe Crest Drive, North Mankato, Minnesota 56003.
www.mycapstone.com

Library of Congress Cataloging-in-Publication Data
is available on the Library of Congress website:
ISBN: 978-1-5435-0607-5 (library binding)
ISBN: 978-1-5435-0615-0 (eBook PDF)

Editorial Credits
Nate LeBoutillier, editor; Brent Slingsby, designer;
Eric Gohl, media research; Laura Manthe, production specialist

Photo Credits
Getty Images: Bill Wippert, 17, Bruce Kluckhohn, 24; Newscom: Cal Sport Media/Anthony Nesmith, 12, 14, Cal Sport Media/Nicholas T. Loverde, 10, Icon Sportswire/Fred Kfoury III, 26, TNS/Adam Cairns, 19, UPI/Mark Goldman, 23, ZUMA Press/Jason Franson, 9; Sports Illustrated: David E. Klutho, cover, 21, 29, Simon Bruty, 5, 7

Design Elements: Shutterstock

All statistics have been updated through the 2016–17 NHL season.

Printed in the United States of America.
010782S18

TABLE OF
CONTENTS

STATS & STORIES

Inside the Numbers

Alex Ovechkin is one of the most feared goal scorers in the National Hockey League (NHL). In seven of his first 12 seasons, the Washington Capitals forward scored more than 50 goals in a season. Six of those times, he was the league leader in goals.

Is Ovechkin the best player in the NHL? Perhaps. Dig deeper into his statistics, and you'll learn more about him. In the 2013–14 season, Ovechkin scored 51 goals, again leading the league. But 24 of his goals came on the power play, and his plus-minus was a very poor minus-35. The Anaheim Ducks' Corey Perry that season scored eight fewer goals than Ovechkin but was plus-32. Meanwhile, the Pittsburgh Penguins' Sidney Crosby won the Hart Trophy as Most Valuable Player (MVP) by scoring 36 goals, assisting on 68 others, and finishing plus-18.

Statistics show the details in sports beyond simple wins and losses. They can explain *why* a team won or lost. They can explain *how* a player rose to a challenge — or failed to do so. They can show *which* players helped or hurt their team's chances at postseason glory. Knowing the numbers and stats will help you better understand the game — and appreciate it too!

Alex Ovechkin, left wing, Washington Capitals

CHAPTER ONE

OFFENSE

Scoring Goals

Sidney Crosby was just 18 years old when he joined the Pittsburgh Penguins, and he made a great first impression. "Sid the Kid" scored 39 goals that season. That's an impressive number for a first-year player, although a far cry from the rookie record of 76 goals set by the Winnipeg Jets' Teemu Selanne.

Scoring goals is the name of the game in hockey. Score more goals than your opponent, and you win! But they don't come easily; hockey games often are low-scoring affairs. In 2016–17 NHL teams scored an average of 2.59 goals per game. Just 25 years earlier, teams were averaging more than three goals each night. But today's goaltenders are bigger and quicker, and their bulky pads cover up much of the goal opening. Nowadays, the best goalies stop almost every open shot. Many goals must be scored by tipping and changing the direction of pucks or by knocking back rebounds off goalie saves.

In 2016–17 Crosby found a way to score more goals than any other NHLer, netting 44. It was the second time in his career he led the league in goals. Crosby finished with a league-leading 51 goals in 2009–10.

Facts and Stats

The Penguins led the NHL in goals in 2016–17 with 278, an average of 3.39 per game. The lowest-scoring team that year was the Colorado Avalanche with 165 goals, or 2.01 per game.

Most Goals, Career

Rank	Player	Teams	Years Played	Goals Scored
01	Wayne Gretzky	Oilers, Kings, Blues, Rangers	1979–99	894
02	Gordie Howe	Red Wings, Whalers	1946–71, 1979–80	801
03	Jaromir Jagr	Penguins, 7 other teams	1990–2017*	765
04	Brett Hull	Blues, 4 other teams	1986–2006	741
05	Marcel Dionne	Red Wings, Kings, Rangers	1971–89	731

* active player

Sidney Crosby, center, Pittsburgh Penguins

Producing Points

Scoring goals in hockey takes teamwork. In fact scoring is so difficult that the sport makes sure to recognize other players who help score the goals. Up to two assists can be awarded for every goal that is scored. An assist is a pass or a touched puck by a teammate that leads to a goal. An assist can also be awarded for a saved shot that turns into a rebound goal for another player.

Assists are so important that they count as scoring points for players. Goals plus assists equals total points, and the player with the most points is the NHL's scoring leader. In 2016–17 dynamic 20-year-old center Connor McDavid of the Edmonton Oilers led the league in assists and points. He finished his second professional season with 30 goals, 70 assists, and 100 points. He also won the Hart Trophy.

That was an impressive season for McDavid. However, Oilers great Wayne Gretzky scored more than 200 points in a season four different times. That includes his single-season record of 215 points (52 goals + 163 assists) in 1985–86.

Facts and Stats

Wayne Gretzky scored so many points that even if his goals were taken away, his assist total (1,963) would still be the NHL's all-time points record.

Connor McDavid, center, Edmonton Oilers

Most Points, Career

Rank	Player	Teams	Years Played
01	Wayne Gretzky	Oilers, Kings, Blues, Rangers	1979–99
02	Jaromir Jagr	Penguins, 7 other teams	1990–2017*
03	Mark Messier	Oilers, Rangers, Canucks	1979–2004
04	Gordie Howe	Red Wings, Whalers	1946–71 1979–80
05	Ron Francis	Whalers, Penguins Hurricanes, Maple Leafs	1981–2004

* active player

Shots

Wayne Gretzky once famously said, "You miss 100 percent of the shots you don't take." In other words, you can't score goals if you don't shoot the puck. Teams try their best to get as many shots on goal as possible. Shots on goal are any shot that has the chance of scoring a goal. They are the sum of goals scored plus saves by the goaltender. Shots that go high or wide or hit the pipe do not count as shots on goal.

In 10 of 11 seasons prior to 2016–17, Alex Ovechkin led the NHL in shots on goal. Ovechkin's streak was broken in 2016–17 by the San Jose Sharks' Brent Burns. Burns got **320** pucks to the net. He also scored **29** goals, the most by a defenseman that season.

Brent Burns, defenseman, San Jose Sharks

By dividing Burns' goals by total shots, you'll find that he had a shooting percentage of **9** percent.

Goals	Total Shots
29	320

$$29 \div 320 = 0.09$$

Burns' shooting percentage was right around the league average. The best shooting percentage that season belonged to the Capitals' T.J. Oshie at 23.1 percent. Oshie scored 33 goals on just 143 shots. In 1980–81, the Kings' Charlie Simmer set the NHL shooting percentage record at 32.8 percent. He scored about one goal for three shots he took, netting 56 goals on 171 shots.

Most Shots on Goal, Career

Rank	Player	Teams	Years Played	Shots on Goal
01	Ray Bourque	Bruins, Avalanche	1979–2001	6,206
02	Jaromir Jagr	Penguins, 7 other teams	1990–2017*	5,605
03	Marcel Dionne	Red Wings, Kings, Rangers	1971–89	5,366
04	Al MacInnis	Flames, Blues	1981–2004	5,157
05	Mike Gartner	Capitals, 4 other teams	1979–98	5,090

* active player

CHAPTER TWO

SPECIAL TEAMS

Power Play!

When the Washington Capitals go on the power play, teams know what's coming. Stopping Alex Ovechkin's blistering shot from the left circle, however, is another matter. For five straight seasons from 2012–13 to 2016–17, Ovechkin led the NHL in power-play goals. In his first 12 seasons, 212 of his 558 career goals (38 percent) came on the power play.

A team is awarded a power play when an opposing player is called for a penalty. In this situation, the penalized team plays with only four players while the other team gets all five of its skaters. Power plays last for the length of the penalty or until a goal is scored.

Jack Eichel, center, Buffalo Sabres

The best power-play units in the NHL score about once every five times they get the player advantage (20 percent). In 2016–17 the team with the best power play was the Buffalo Sabres, led by Jack Eichel, Sam Reinhart, Kyle Okposo, Ryan O'Reilly, and Rasmus Ristolainen. The rate is measured by dividing the number of power-play goals by the number of power-play chances. The Sabres scored **57** goals on **233** chances for **24.5** percent.

Goals	Chances
57	233

$$57 \div 233 = 0.245$$

Facts and Stats

The 1977–78 Montreal Canadiens had the best power play ever, scoring an amazing 31.88 percent of the time. In the 1997–98 season, the Tampa Bay Lightning had the worst all-time power play. They scored just 9.35 percent of the time.

Most Power-Play Goals, Career

Rank	Player	Teams	Years Played	Power-Play Goals
01	Dave Andreychuk	Sabres, 5 other teams	1982–2006	274
02	Brett Hull	Blues, 4 other teams	1986–2006	265
03	Teemu Selanne	Jets, Ducks, Sharks, Avalanche	1992–2014	255
04	Phil Esposito	Blackhawks, Bruins, Rangers	1963–81	249
05	Luc Robitaille	Kings, Penguins, Rangers, Red Wings	1986–2006	247

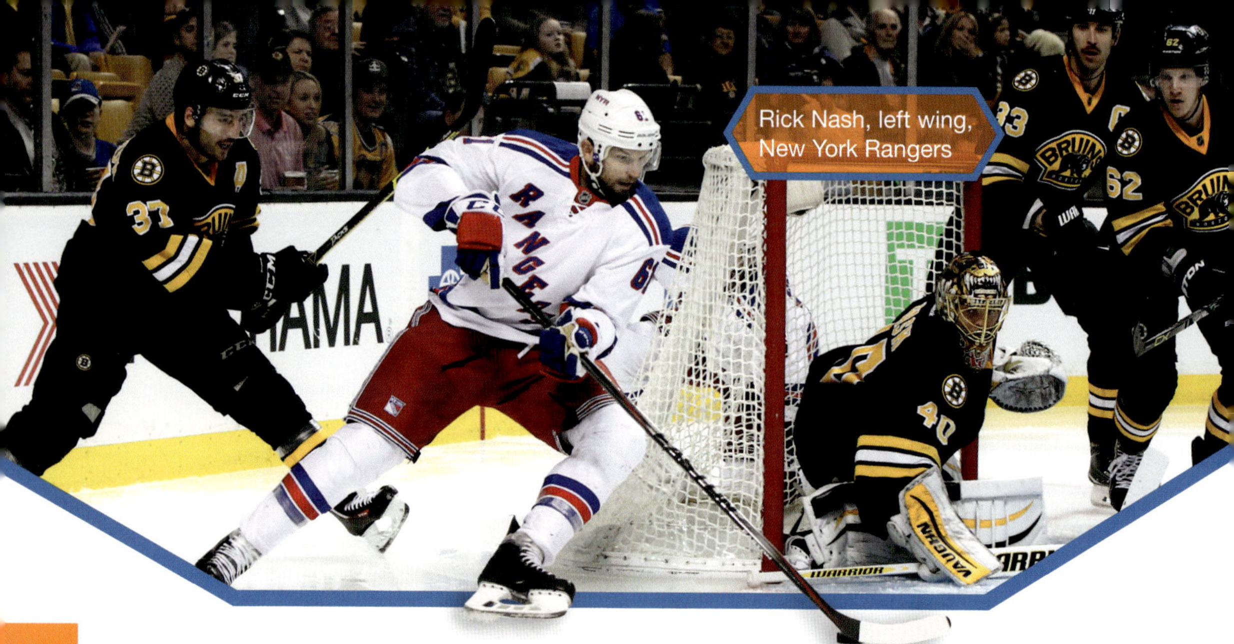

Rick Nash, left wing, New York Rangers

Playing Short-Handed

When a player is called for a penalty, he has to sit in the penalty box as a punishment. As he waits, he hopes that his teammates on the penalty kill can bail him out by preventing a power-play goal. If they keep the other team off the scoreboard, the penalized player gets to skate back out on the ice once his two minutes are up. No harm done.

A penalty kill's success is measured as a percentage. Just divide the number of successful kills by the total number of opponents' power plays. The best teams kill penalties at a rate of 80 percent or better. The Boston Bruins led the NHL at 85.7 percent in 2016–17. They allowed just 38 goals on 266 chances, killing the penalty 228 times.

Kills	Chances
228	266

$$228 \div 266 = 0.857$$

Even better for a penalty-killing unit is when it can score while short-handed. Short-handed goals are rare. Of the NHL's current players, the New York Rangers' Rick Nash is one of the best. At the tender age of 19, Nash led the NHL in 2003–04 with 41 total goals while playing for the Columbus Blue Jackets. As of 2017, he had 22 career short-handed goals, one of the best totals of active players.

Facts and Stats

In 2010 the Bruins scored three short-handed goals during the same penalty kill. The goals came in a span of just 64 seconds.

Most Short-Handed Goals, Career

Rank	Player	Teams	Years Played
01	Wayne Gretzky	Oilers, Kings, Blues, Rangers	1979–99
02	Mark Messier	Oilers, Rangers, Canucks	1979–2004
03	Steve Yzerman	Red Wings	1983–2006
04	Mario Lemieux	Penguins	1984–97 2000–06
05	Butch Goring	Kings, Islanders, Bruins	1969–85

To the Penalty Box

Penalties are part of hockey. Whether penalties are called for hooking, holding, cross-checking, slashing, elbowing, or roughing, they are going to happen. Players' penalties are measured not in the number that they take but in the sum of the number of penalized minutes their broken rules are worth. The statistic is called penalties in minutes (PIM).

The most-common penalties such as holding or cross-checking are called minors. They are worth two minutes each. Even if a power-play goal is scored, the full two minutes are added to the player's stats. Major penalties such as spearing or fighting, which are for more-dangerous plays, are worth five minutes each. Misconducts, including penalties that force the player to leave the game, are worth 10 minutes.

Bruins defenseman Zdeno Chara ranks second among current players in career penalty minutes. He's spent 1,779 minutes — almost 30 hours! — in the box. In 2016–17, the Ottawa Senators' Mark Borowiecki had 154 penalty minutes, which led the league that year. But that was nothing compared to Dave Schultz in 1974–75. That season, Schultz set the single-season record with 472 minutes in penalties.

Facts and Stats

The Los Angeles Kings' Randy Holt was called for nine penalties totaling 67 minutes in a single game in 1979. In 1991 the Bruins' Chris "Knuckles" Nilan was penalized 10 times for 42 minutes.

Most Penalty Minutes, Career

Rank	Player	Teams	Years Played
01	Tiger Williams	Maple Leafs, 4 other teams	1974–88
02	Dale Hunter	Nordiques, Capitals, Avalanche	1980–99
03	Tie Domi	Maple Leafs, Rangers, Jets	1989–2006
04	Marty McSorley	Kings, 5 other teams	1983–2000
05	Bob Probert	Red Wings, Blackhawks	1985–2002

Zdeno Chara, defenseman, Boston Bruins

CHAPTER THREE

GOALTENDING

Save Percentage

The Columbus Blue Jackets were one of the surprise teams of the 2016–17 season. They improved their win total from the previous season by 16 games and made the playoffs for the first time in three years. A big reason for their improvement was goaltending. Sergei Bobrovsky proved tough to beat all season long. He stopped **93.1** percent of opponents' shots on goal by making **1,727** saves on **1,854** shot attempts, the best in the NHL.

Saves	Shot Attempts
1,727	1,854

1,727 ÷ 1,854 = 0.931

Save percentage is calculated by dividing the number of saves a goalie makes by the number of shots on goal he sees. A save percentage of .900 or more is considered good. Get up into the .930 range, like Bobrovsky, and you're in rare company.

Save percentage isn't a perfect stat. It includes all situations (even-strength, power play, penalty kill), as well as shots from anywhere on the ice. Equal weight is given to a low-percentage wrister from the blue line as it is to a high-percentage breakaway by a great scorer.

Facts and Stats

Only two players have finished a regular season at or above the .940 mark. The Ottawa Senators' Craig Anderson did it in 2012–13 with a .941 percentage. The St. Louis Blues' Brian Elliott hit .940 in 2011–12.

Best Save Percentage, Career

Rank	Player	Teams	Years Played	Shots on Goal
01	Tuukka Rask	Bruins	2007–2017*	.923
02	Dominik Hasek	Blackhawks, Sabres, Red Wings, Senators	1990–2008	.922
03	Cory Schneider	Canucks, Devils	2008–2017*	.922
04	Braden Holtby	Capitals	2010–2017*	.922
05	Carey Price	Canadiens	2008–2017*	.920

* active player

Sergei Bobrovsky, goalie, Columbus Blue Jackets

Goals-Against Average

The Chicago Blackhawks were the number one seed in the Western Conference when the 2017 Stanley Cup playoffs began. But in the playoffs, they ran into hot goaltender Pekka Rinne of the eighth-seeded Nashville Predators. Rinne allowed just three goals in four games to help the Preds sweep the series. He carried his team all the way to the Finals before the Predators lost against the Pittsburgh Penguins.

Rinne finished the playoffs with a goals-against average of 1.96. Goals-against average (GAA) is the number of goals allowed by a goaltender per 60 minutes of play — the length of a regulation game.

Goalies may play more than 60 minutes if a game goes to overtime. Or he may play fewer minutes if he is replaced or taken off the ice. To figure out a goalie's goals-against average, first divide the number of goals allowed by the number of minutes played. Then multiply that number by 60, the full number of minutes in a game.

In those four games against Chicago, Rinne played 256 minutes and 44 seconds while allowing just 3 goals. So he had a GAA of 0.70.

Goals Allowed: 3

Minutes Played: 256.73

$$(3 \div 256.73) \times 60 = 0.70$$

Facts and Stats

In 1928–29 the Montreal Canadiens' George Hainsworth had a 0.92 GAA. It was the only time a goalie finished a season below 1.00. That was a different era, however. Hockey rules of the time made scoring more difficult for offenses.

Lowest Goals-Against Average, Career

Rank	Player	Teams	Years Played	Goals-Against Average
01	Alec Connell	Senators, Falcons, Maroons, Americans	1924–37	1.91
02	George Hainsworth	Canadiens, Maple Leafs	1926–37	1.93
03	Charlie Gardiner	Blackhawks	1927–34	2.02
04	Lorne Chabot	Rangers, Maple Leafs, 4 other teams	1926–37	2.03
05	Tiny Thompson	Bruins, Red Wings	1928–40	2.08

Pekka Rinne, goalie, Nashville Predators

Wins

Like pitchers in baseball, goaltenders get credit for wins and losses. Although hockey is a team game, many eyes are on the goalie. A couple of spine-bending saves can make all the difference between victory and defeat.

In recent years, no goaltender has won quite like Braden Holtby of the Capitals. By winning 42 games in 2016–17, he became just the third goalie in NHL history to string together three straight 40-win seasons. His 48 wins a season earlier tied the league record set by Martin Brodeur of the New Jersey Devils in 2006–07.

No goalie win is quite as thrilling as a shutout, when a goaltender allows no pucks to get past him. Holtby had nine shutouts in 2016–17. The modern-era shutout record belongs to Tony Esposito, who had 15 clean sheets in 1969–70 for the Blackhawks. However, in the league's early years, George Hainsworth once recorded 22 shutouts.

Most Wins, Career

Rank	Player	Teams	Years Played	Goals-Against Average
01	Martin Brodeur	Devils, Blues	1991–2015	691
02	Patrick Roy	Canadiens, Avalanche	1984–2003	551
03	Ed Belfour	Blackhawks, 4 other teams	1988–2007	484
04	Curtis Joseph	Blues, 5 other teams	1989–2009	454
05	Roberto Luongo	Islanders, Panthers, Canucks	1999–2017*	453

* active player

Braden Holtby, goalie, Washington Capitals

Most Shutouts, Career

Rank	Player	Teams	Years Played	Shots on Goal
01	Martin Brodeur	Devils, Blues	1991–2015	125
02	Terry Sawchuck	Red Wings, 4 other teams	1949–70	103
03	George Hainsworth	Canadiens, Maple Leafs	1926–37	94
04	Glenn Hall	Red Wings, Blackhawks, Blues	1952–71	84
05	Jacques Plante	Canadiens, 5 other teams	1952–75	82

CHAPTER FOUR

PUCK POSSESSION

Plus-Minus

Defenseman Ryan Suter and forward Jason Zucker were key players in the Minnesota Wild's outstanding 2016–17 season. By the end of the year, the duo was tied for the league lead in plus-minus at plus-34. That meant each player was on the ice for 34 more of the Wild's goals than opponents' goals.

Plus-minus is one way to measure the impact players have while they're on the ice. A player gets a plus if his team scores, and he gets a minus if the opponent scores. No plus or minus is tallied for power-play goals (but they are for short-handed scores).

Jason Zucker (left) and Ryan Suter, defensemen, Minnesota Wild

Hockey is a game played in shifts. Groups of three forwards, called lines, and pairs of defensemen move back and forth from the bench to the ice. A plus or a minus is highly dependent on how one's group plays. Because of that, some people believe the stat is not an accurate measurement of a player's performance. In 2016–17 the Dallas Stars missed the playoffs despite having two of the top 25 scorers in Tyler Seguin and Jamie Benn. Seguin had 72 points that season but finished with a minus-15. Benn had 69 points and was minus-9.

Facts and Stats

The best single-season plus-minus of all time was set by Bobby Orr in 1970–71. The Boston Bruins defenseman finished the season with plus-124.

Best Plus-Minus, Career

Rank	Player	Teams	Years Played
01	Larry Robinson	Canadiens, Kings	1972–92
02	Bobby Orr	Bruins, Blackhawks	1966–79
03	Ray Bourque	Bruins, Avalanche	1979–2001
04	Wayne Gretzky	Oilers, Kings, Blues, Rangers	1979–99
05	Bobby Clarke	Flyers	1969–84

Patrice Bergeron, center, Boston Bruins

Advanced Stats

Plus-minus doesn't consider factors such as good (or bad) goaltending or mistakes made by teammates. It also may be unfair to defensive players who have the tough task of checking the other teams' superstars every night.

In recent years, advanced statistics have been introduced to better judge a player's performance on the ice. More often than not, the stats show that teams that possess the puck the most tend to win more games. And players who can help a team control the puck are more valuable.

A stat called Corsi measures all attempted shots for and against a team while a player (or team) is on the ice. The stat is named after its inventor, a goaltending coach named Jim Corsi. In 2016–17, the Bruins' Patrice Bergeron had the best Corsi percentage in the league at 62.1 percent. When he was on the ice, the Bruins attempted 1,868 shots, and their opponents attempted 1,141.

Having a good Corsi number is all about controlling the puck.

Corsi Leaders, 2016-17

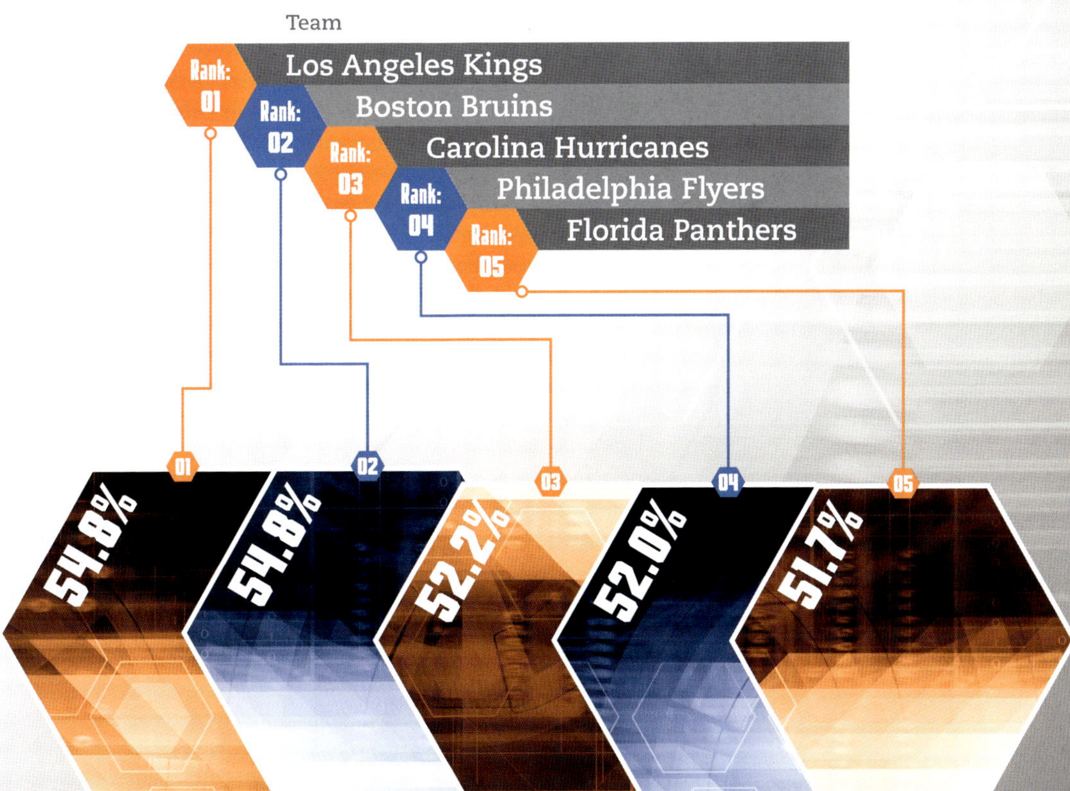

Faceoffs

When the Chicago Blackhawks need to get possession of the puck, they like to send their captain, Jonathan Toews, onto the ice to take the faceoff. And why not? Toews has led the Blackhawks to three Stanley Cup championships with his stellar play. That most certainly includes his dominance in the faceoff circle.

Faceoffs take place before every period, after every goal, and after every stoppage of play. Toews has been one of the NHL's very best faceoff men throughout his career. In 2015–16, he led the NHL in faceoff percentage. That season, Toews won 921 of 1,573 faceoffs for a 58.6 winning percentage.

Faceoffs Won	Total Faceoffs
921	1,573

$$921 \div 1{,}573 = 0.586$$

The advantage of winning faceoffs is not just about winning draws. It's also about where and when a player wins faceoffs. Statisticians keep track of those too. They record faceoffs in the offensive, defensive, and neutral zones. They look at them during even-strength, power-play, and penalty-kill situations. And they really note them late in games when a team is ahead or behind.

The difference between winning a one-goal game in regulation and facing the opponent in overtime just might come down to a faceoff. Can someone win that defensive-zone draw and give his team the puck in order to protect that late lead?

Faceoff Leaders, 2016-17

Rank	Player	Team	Faceoff Win Percentage
01	Matt Duchene	Avalanche	62.6%
02	Antoine Vermette	Ducks	62.3%
03	Patrice Bergeron	Bruins	60.1 %
04	Jordan Staal	Hurricanes	59.1 %
05	Ryan O'Reilly	Sabres	58.0 %

Jonathan Toews, center, Chicago Blackhawks

GLOSSARY

assist — a pass or touch of the puck that sets up a goal

career — a job or profession someone does for a long time; in sports, all of the years a player plays

center — a position in hockey, a forward who usually plays in the middle of the ice

cross-checking — a penalty called when a player uses two hands to hit an opponent with the shaft of his stick

draw — another word for faceoff

misconduct — wrong or poor behavior; in hockey, a 10-minute penalty that does not include a power play

penalty kill — when one team prevents another team's power play from scoring

possession — having or owning something; in hockey, having control of the puck

power play — situation where one team has more players on the ice than the other team for a period of time because of a penalty

short-handed — playing with one or more fewer players on the ice because of penalties

READ MORE

Doeden, Matt. *Sidney Crosby: Hockey Superstar*. Sports Illustrated Kids. Super Star Athletes. North Mankato, Minn.: Capstone Press, 2012.

Frederick Shane. *Hockey Stats and the Stories Behind Them*. Sports Illustrated Kids: Stats and Stories. North Mankato, Minn.: Capstone Press, 2016.

Zweig, Eric. *Great Goalies (Hockey Hall of Fame Kids)*. Richmond Hill, Ontario, Canada: Firefly Books, 2014.

INTERNET SITES

Use FactHound to find internet sites related to this book.

Visit **www.facthound.com**

Just type in **9781543506075** and go.

INDEX